# BRUNO

## These don't belong to you

Story and Illustrations by
Tony Costanzo

To order additional copies of this book, contact:
Xlibris
844-714-8691
www.Xlibris.com
Orders@Xlibris.com

ISBN: 978-1-9845-8650-6 (sc)
ISBN: 978-1-9845-8649-0 (hc)
ISBN: 978-1-9845-8648-3 (e)

Print information available on the last page

Rev. date: 09/01/2020

# BRUNO

## THESE DON'T BELONG TO YOU!

BY

ANTHONY COSTANZO

My name is Tony Costanzo. I am a retired school teacher. I live in Rye, NH, a small town bordering the Atlantic Ocean. My wife, JoAnn and I have been married for over 50 years. We have three wonderful children, daughter in law and son in law and a new granddaughter.

I have enjoyed creative writing. Two dogs Max and Billy always seem to find an adventure. This story's theme is about all the stuffed animals and dolls that were an important part of our early lives. We always felt safer with them in our arms. Today they may be in the attic or on a top shelf. This story hopefully makes us all realize how valuable they still are.

It was just a regular morning for our two favorite dogs, Max and Billy. The plan was a trip downtown to their old friend Oscar's Repair Shop and then a visit to the kids' park .

Old Oscar was fun to watch. He was a tall man with thick glasses, a mustache and above all a kind heart. Oscar could sew, patch, glue, rebuild, clean and fix any kids' stuffed animal or doll. Best of all Oscar always stopped to give Max and Billy special attention and tasty doggie treats. "Well, welcome to my two special visitors", Oscar would say.

The shop was always a busy, action filled place. Boxes of stuffing, plastic eyes, spools of thread, glue tubes, different types of hair and repair tools were everywhere.

Moms and even kids would drop off their lovable dolls and stuffed animals for a serious repair or just a makeover.

Today seemed very different. While the dogs were enjoying their usual cookie treats, Oscar was a little busier than normal. A wire crate full of damaged fuzzy friends, mascots, and dolls was on the floor of the shop. Oscar was quietly promising little four year old Emma that he'd be able to fix her little kitty cat "Bee Bee's "loose eye and not to worry.

Finally, Oscar stopped and talked to Max and Billy. " More and more cuddly friends have been coming in", he said "They have bite marks and are torn up," he went on, "it even looks like some of them have been dragged on the ground."

Oscar could not figure out how this was happening. It was not damage done by kids.

"There is something else that I want you both to see," he whispered softly. Then he brought the dogs into the next room where he kept his supplies and poster messages.

The entire wall was covered with posters of missing little stuffed animals and dolls. A lot of them were just added in the past few days. Many were last seen at the children's playground. Oscar pointed to a poster of Thunder the Elephant, remembering when he was brand new.

Now, old Oscar sometimes could work miracles. He could re-stuff Tubby the Bear, put eyes back on Doll Baby, and sew buttons on Snowy the Rabbit. One time he even made Squishy the Giraffe's long flat neck look like brand new. Oscar had a great supply of spare parts like plastic arms, eyes, legs, hair, stuffing, and clothing. All meant nothing if they couldn't be used to fix these missing cuddly friends. The dogs listened carefully. They were going to the children's park next and hoped to look around for clues. Something was going on? They had to find out more.

Watching the kids play at the park was like seeing an action packed movie. Little people running, jumping, sliding, swinging and chasing each other, all in super-fast motion. Billy barked to Max, "My eyes go left, then go right and back again". It was a joy listening to their laughter. Somebody once said that children have a full time work job called running and playing.

Moms and Dads just watch, but inside them is a kid that wants to play too. They have to remind the kids to be respectful and safe around all the equipment. Backpacks, baby carriages, bikes, bags with snacks, and kids' stuffed animals were everywhere.

Max ran into his old friend, Basil from Puppy Day Care School. Basil had been at the park most of the day. He told Max and Billy about some of the strange things that he had seen just this past week.

Dogs are famous for their extra senses to notice things and see more details. Stringy the Worm was left alone on the red bench. Doll Baby fell out of little Suzie's carriage, as her mom was looking the other way and did not even stop. Somebody left Snowball the Cat on the ground by the big tree.

They watched little Amy Lou on the seahorse spring ride singing a song. She never saw her special friend, Ziggy the Zebra, bounce out of her backpack on to the ground.

The three dogs were amazed when they saw Mister Lazy the turtle upside down on the grass near them. Basil saw one eye loose and stuffing everywhere. Then Billy barked out, "Look at those drag lines, something has tried to pull him along!"

All this was very strange to look at. Soon they were about to find out exactly what happened!

Things started in motion quickly. First in the distance they heard Amy Lou's Mom shout out, "Time for lunch, Please get Ziggy and let's go!" All Amy Lou could say was, "Ziggy all gone!" and she saw something flash right past her as the ground shook around the ride.

A funny looking creature low to the ground darted by Max and Billy. Ziggy was dangling from its wide mouth. It was very stocky and muscular with a wrinkled face that bounced all over the place. Then like a thundering buffalo it turned right toward the park's exit leading to a pathway behind the city's buildings. The dogs knew that this is what has been going on the past week.

Max and Billy saw the creature ahead in the distance. They didn't waste a second and started following it out of the park and toward the city alley way.

It was a messy alley path with junk, trash cans, cardboard boxes, tires and rusty old pieces of things everywhere. Billy with his big sensitive nose even picked up the smelly scent of old garbage bags. Poor little Max just missed stepping on a piece of broken glass. This is where people threw things away that they didn't want. Being in between all the city's big buildings also blocked out the sun and made it a bit dark.

Max and Billy really couldn't keep up with the creature. Thankfully, they were able to follow a trail of stuffing that was falling out of Ziggy. Maybe this was Ziggy's way of helping them rescue him?

The creature made a sharp turn just past a big green dumpster near some garbage cans and then seemed to stop running.

Both dogs were huffing and puffing as they stopped at the side of a big green rubbish dumpster. Billy with his long neck looked around it's rusty corner. Max as always was right by his side. They could see that the creature had stopped. It was settled in what looked like a homemade nest filled with stuffed animals and dolls! It was neatly packed and looked cozy. They now knew what happened to all the kids' stuffed animals and dolls.

It was one of the saddest sights the dogs had ever seen. This stocky, tough looking creature with an empty look in it's eyes was with it's ONLY FRIENDS! The nest was a pile of teddy bears, stuffed bunny rabbits, kitty cats, a giraffe, several dolls, Leo the Lama, Thunder the elephant and now a zebra named Ziggy. As he got a closer look, Max whispered to Billy, "That creature is a bulldog and the name on the tray says, Bruno! "What to do next?

Within minutes, Max and Billy were telling their story to the one person who could fix this problem, Oscar. "This explains everything", said a surprised Oscar.

Then something very amazing happened. Oscar's elbow accidentally knocked over a stuffed animal from his countertop. Unbelievable, it was a toy bulldog that had been in the repair shop for a long long time because nobody claimed it. How did this happen? Max and Billy starred at each other in shock! They thought this is a miracle and it's exactly what Bruno would love to have.

It didn't take Oscar long to quick brush and clean up the stuffed little bulldog. He put it in a nice box with a fancy bow and wrote the name Bruno!

"Okay boys let's get going before he moves to a different place, lead the way", Oscar said.

Soon they were at the spot in the alley. The dogs waited as Oscar approached Bruno's nest very slowly! Oscar was thinking to himself how he repaired stuffed animals and here is this lonely creature who loves them too. All kids looked to them for friendship and feeling safer with them around.

Oscar spoke in a soft voice as he opened the box for Bruno to see. Suddenly every layer of that wrinkled flat face slid upward into a happy smile. Oscar put the stuffed puppy bulldog down near Bruno. Then he said," Would you like me to take care of you? You can live in my repair shop."

Bruno barked and barked out in pure joy! "YES" was written all over his bulldog face. It was the most special time ever. Max and Billy watched as Bruno followed Oscar back to the repair shop.

The next morning couldn't get here soon enough. Both dogs made their way downtown to Oscar's Shop. They knew he would be real busy, so they just peeked in from the street window.

Oscar had brought back all the damaged stuffed animals and dolls in an old metal shopping cart he found in the alley. You could see that he was going full force fixing and repairing them.

Yesterday in the alley, he told the dogs that he would plan a special day at the kids' park. He hoped to return everything to their young owners. That message board at the shop would be a big help. Little Ziggy the Zebra was his first patient.

Things seemed cheerful now. Oscar had a joyful, happy friend feasting on a nice breakfast by his side. Bruno wasn't lonely anymore. He had a real home.

BRUNO

What a special day at the kids' park, thanks to old Oscar! Every dolly, teddy bear, bunny rabbit, giraffe, elephant and stuffed animal looked spanking new and ready to return back home.

The children got into a line as Oscar held up each treasure. First in line was Little Amy Lou. She held tightly on to her Ziggy the Zebra crying out, "You will be safe with me from now on, I promise!"

On and on the line moved. Snowball the cat, then Leo Lama were some of the many now back together with their little owners.

Joy and happiness were everywhere.

Here's the best part of this story. WATCHING ALL THIS WAS A BEAMING BRUNO JUST SO HAPPY TO BE LOVED AND ACCEPTED!

Printed in the United States
By Bookmasters